From a child of the 70s to everyone else—A. J.

For Virginia Peters, a true ray
of sunshine who always seems to shine brightest
when my skies are their cloudiest—L. L.

THE DAY RAY GOT AWAY

Angela Johnson · Luke LaMarca

SIMON & SCHUSTER BOOKS FOR YOUNG READERS

New York   London   Toronto   Sydney

The day Ray got away, the morning sun rose orange and yellow over the balloon warehouse.

The Big Fat Cartoon Cat was half inflated.
The Superheroes were all puffed up.
The Moose was complaining about antler space.
And the new balloon was zooming around
trying to be the first in line.

That morning Ray woke
with a smile.
(He always did.)

He quietly got inflated,
looked around the warehouse,

The day Ray got away,
the Big Fat Cartoon Cat laughed
and the Superheroes flexed.
The Moose worried. Would his antlers snag on
  a building?

But the line-jumping new kid floated slowly
  over to Ray and said,
"What about today?"

So he told her.

"I've been here a long time, so today's the day."
Then he smiled at the new kid.
(He always did.)

It was rare for a balloon like Ray,
who had been good for years,
to decide that "today was the day."
So the other balloons called him a dreamer.

But two hours later, when the warehouse doors slid back
and Ray peeked out,
the other balloons held their breaths.

(What else were they gonna do?)

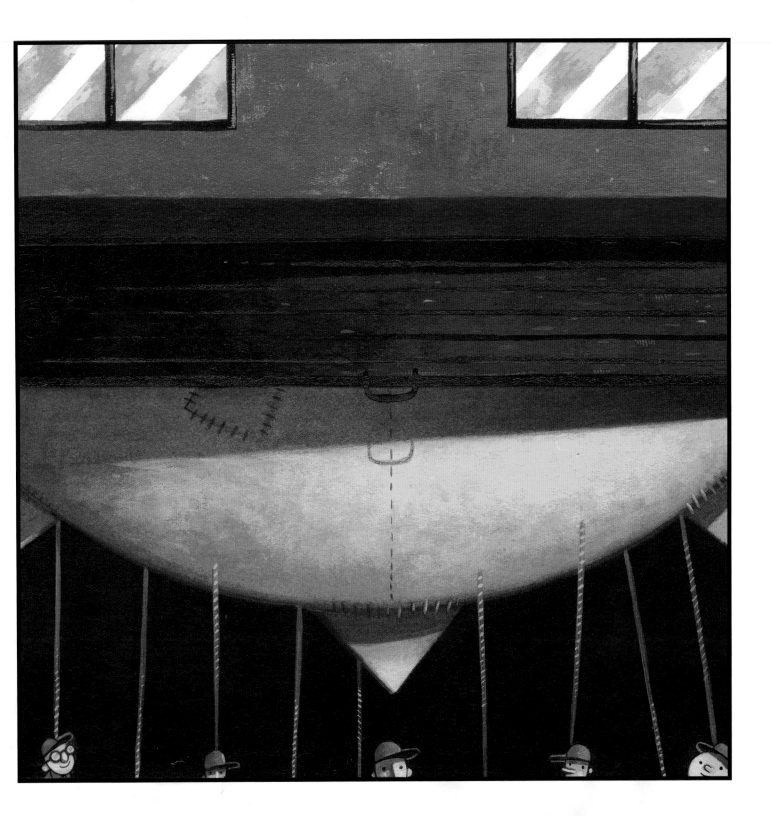

The day Ray got away, thousands of people lined the sidewalks to watch the balloon parade.

And they weren't disappointed. The balloons all knew their jobs.

The Superheroes flexed.
The new kid bounced.

The Big Fat Cartoon Cat smirked. And even the Moose had fun and didn't get hung up (on a building or anything else).

But then a shout rang out,
and ropes began to . . .

SNAP,
"He's loose!"
"Try to grab his foot, er, ray!"
SNAP,
SNAP.
KMP
But it was too late.

That day the parade was a disaster:

clowns everywhere,

bands backed up downtown,

the parade marshal in hysterics,

paper flowers as far as the eye could see,

. . . and Ray,
shining bright, smiling (he always did).

The handlers told a reporter,
"There'd been talk in the warehouse.
We were due for a balloon uprising.
I guess today was the day."

That day the other balloons felt freer
   and pulled their own ropes harder,
and were a little difficult to get back
   to the warehouse.
The Superheroes wouldn't stop flexing.

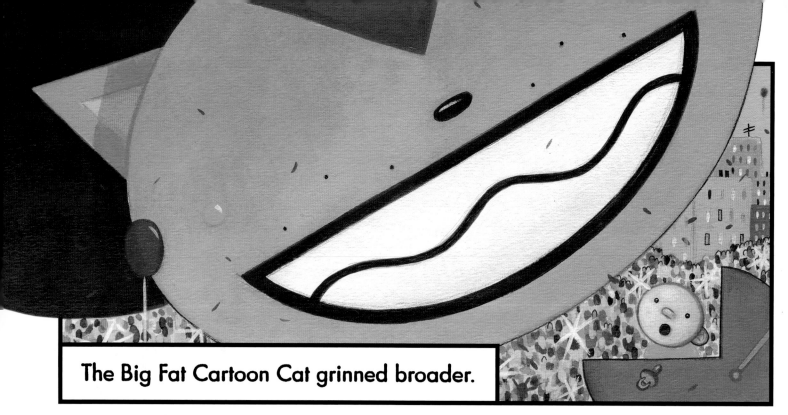

The Big Fat Cartoon Cat grinned broader.

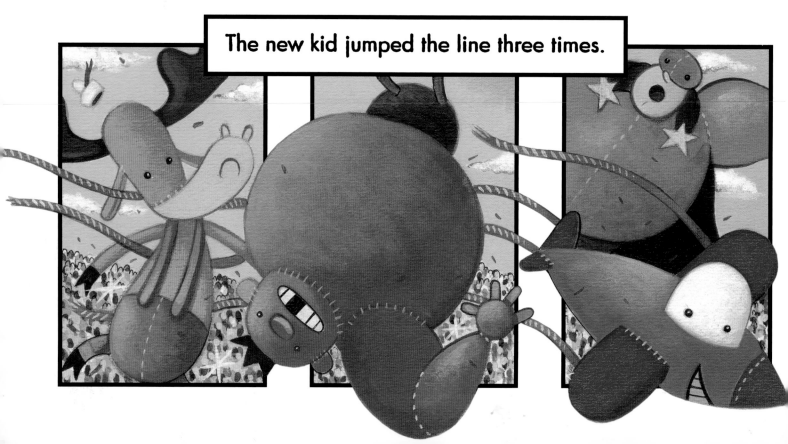

The new kid jumped the line three times.

And the Moose intentionally snagged himself on the tallest building he could find.

And Ray? Well, over by the river one of the handlers almost caught him.

But Ray got away.

SIMON & SCHUSTER BOOKS FOR YOUNG READERS

An imprint of Simon & Schuster Children's Publishing Division

1230 Avenue of the Americas, New York, New York 10020

Text copyright © 2010 by Angela Johnson

Illustrations copyright © 2010 by Luke LaMarca

For information about special discounts for bulk purchases, please contact

Simon & Schuster Special Sales at 1-866-506-1949 or business@simonandschuster.com.

The Simon & Schuster Speakers Bureau can bring authors to your live event. For more information or to book an event,

contact the Simon & Schuster Speakers Bureau at 1-866-248-3049 or visit our website at www.simonspeakers.com.

Book design by Jessica Handelman

The text for this book is set in Graham Bold.

The illustrations for this book are rendered in acrylic paint.

Manufactured in China

0110 SCP

2 4 6 8 10 9 7 5 3 1

Johnson, Angela, 1961–

The day Ray got away / Angela Johnson; illustrated by Luke LaMarca.—1st ed.

p. cm.

Summary: A parade balloon shaped like a sun breaks free of his strings and flies away from the other balloons.

ISBN 978-0-689-87375-1

[1. Balloons—Fiction. 2. Parades—Fiction.] I. LaMarca, Luke, ill. II. Title.

PZ7.J629Ray 2010

[E]—dc22

2008015864

first
edition